4/06

Keys and Clues
for Benny

CREATED BY

Gertrude Chandler Warner

ILLUSTRATED BY

Kay Life

Albert Whitman & Company

Morton Grove, Illinois

You will also want to read:

Meet the Boxcar Children

A Present for Grandfather

Benny's New Friend

The Magic Show Mystery

Benny Goes into Business

Watch Runs Away

The Secret under the Tree

Benny's Saturday Surprise

Sam Makes Trouble

Watch, the Superdog!

Library of Congress Cataloging-in-Publication Data
Warner, Gertrude Chandler, 1890-
Keys and clues for Benny / created by Gertrude Chandler Warner;
illustrated by Kay Life.
p. cm. — (The Adventures of Benny & Watch; #11)
Summary: When Benny Alden sees a set of keys that were lost
at the library, he follows clues to find the owner.
ISBN 0-8075-4172-9 (pbk.)
[1. Lost and found possessions—Fiction. 2. Locks and keys—Fiction.]
I. Life, Kay, ill. II. Title. PZ7.W244Ke 2004
[E]—dc22 2003015144

Henry

Jessie

Grandfather

Violet

Watch

Benny

The Boxcar Children

Henry, Jessie, Violet, and Benny Alden are orphans. They are supposed to live with their grandfather, but they have heard that he is mean.

So the children run away and live in an old red boxcar. They find a dog, and Benny names him Watch.

When Grandfather finds them, the children see that he is not mean at all. They happily go to live with him. And, as a surprise, Grandfather brings the boxcar along!

Henry, Jessie, and Violet were going to the library.

"Can Watch and I come?" Benny asked. "I'm done with my book!"

"Already?" Violet asked.

Jessie laughed. "Okay. Go get ready."

Benny found his book. But he couldn't find his cool new baseball cap.

"I lost it," said Benny sadly.
"I have an idea," said Jessie.
"Let's go to the library."

At the library, Benny and his
sisters went up to the front desk.
    The man there brought out a big
box that said "Lost and Found."
In it were sunglasses, three mittens,
a set of keys,...

and Benny's cap!

"Wow! How did you know it was here?" he asked Jessie.

"It was a good guess," she said.

"I wonder who lost those keys," Benny said.

"I wish we knew," said the man. "They've been here for a week."

"Maybe I can help find the person who lost them," Benny said. He knew losing things wasn't fun.

"Hmm," said the man. "You can try. But the keys need to stay here.

"Can you draw them?" Benny asked Violet.

Violet opened her notebook
and drew the keys.

The key chain had two rings and three tags. One tag said "State Bank." The second said "I ♥ Donuts." The third was a blue tag shaped like a little dog.

There were four keys. One key was very strange.

Benny went outside with the drawing. "I'll take Watch now," he told Henry.

Benny saw a girl at the bike rack. She began to unlock her bike with a key. He had an idea.

"May I see your key?" he asked. Her key was the same kind as the strange one in the drawing. Benny had his first clue!

"Whoever lost those keys has a bike," he thought.

But now the bike rack was empty. Benny would need a better clue. He looked at the drawing again.

One of the tags read "State Bank."
Another clue!
    State Bank was right down the
street. Benny and Watch peeked
inside. They saw a long line of people.

They also saw a big basket with a sign. "Free Key Rings," it read.

"That clue wasn't very good," he told Watch. "Too many people have that key ring. And we're looking for just one person."

Watch began to pull on his leash.
"What is it, Watch?" Benny
asked. "Another clue?" He let
Watch lead the way.

But Watch had found another dog. He just wanted to play.

Benny sighed. "I'm glad you found a friend," he said. "But we are trying to find *clues*. Come on!"

The second key ring tag said
"I ❤ Donuts." "Whoever lost the
keys loves donuts," Benny
thought. He liked this clue! He
went next door to the bakery.

A woman was leaving the bakery.
"Sorry, they just closed," she said.
Oh, no! Benny was out of clues.
And it was time to go home.

At home, Watch snuggled close, and Benny felt a little better.

They all looked at the drawing again.

"This person loves donuts," said Henry. "Just like you, Benny."

"I wonder what else this person
loves," said Violet.

Benny looked at the blue tag.
He had another idea.

The next day, Benny wanted to go downtown again.

"What will you look for?" Grandfather asked.

"Donuts," Benny said.

The Aldens walked downtown. Benny and Watch led the way. They walked right past the bakery.

"Aren't we going in?" asked Jessie.

"No," said Benny. They walked past the bank, too.

They went to the park
where Benny and Watch
liked to go on walks.
  They saw a woman walking her
little dog. Watch knew this dog!

And Benny knew this woman from the bakery!

"Did you lose your keys last week?" Benny asked the woman.

The woman's eyes got wide. "Oh, my goodness," she said. "Yes, I did!"

"I've been looking for you! I'm Benny Alden," he said. "Your keys are at the library."

"I'm Mrs. Yee," said the woman. "And my dog is Donuts. Thank you so much! How did you know how to find me?"

"It was a good guess!" said Benny.
Jessie hugged him. "A very good
guess," she said.